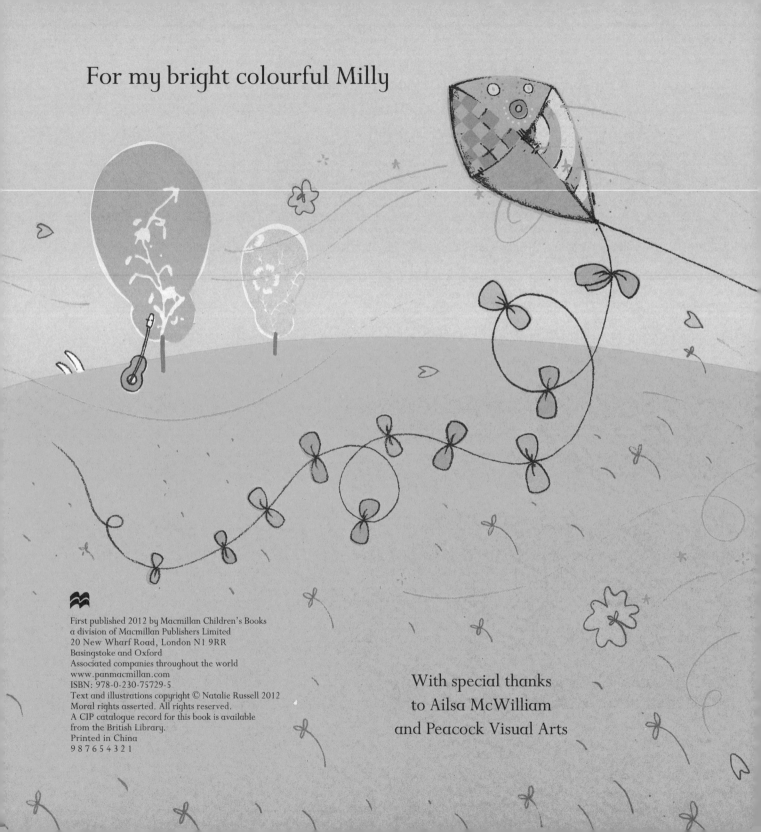

For my bright colourful Milly

First published 2012 by Macmillan Children's Books
a division of Macmillan Publishers Limited
20 New Wharf Road, London N1 9RR
Basingstoke and Oxford
Associated companies throughout the world
www.panmacmillan.com
ISBN: 978-0-230-75729-5
Text and illustrations copyright © Natalie Russell 2012
Moral rights asserted. All rights reserved.
A CIP catalogue record for this book is available
from the British Library.
Printed in China
9 8 7 6 5 4 3 2 1

With special thanks
to Ailsa McWilliam
and Peacock Visual Arts

natalie russell

rabbits in the park

a book of colours

MACMILLAN CHILDREN'S BOOKS

It's a very windy day! Brown Rabbit is outside flying his **green** kite.

snap!

But the string breaks and it whirls away!

ZZZZZZZZZ

Shhh… Little Rabbit is fast asleep
under the blossom tree.

Whoops!
There blows her pretty **pink** bag.

Honey Rabbit's **red** windmill spins
round and round in the wind.

whirrrrrrrrrr

whirrrrrrrrrr

But it goes so fast it spins away!

Poor Grey Rabbit, he hasn't caught a single fish.
And the wind is causing so much trouble!

swish

It's taken his bright **blue** hat!

Rust Rabbit is by the pond too,
sailing his **yellow** boat.

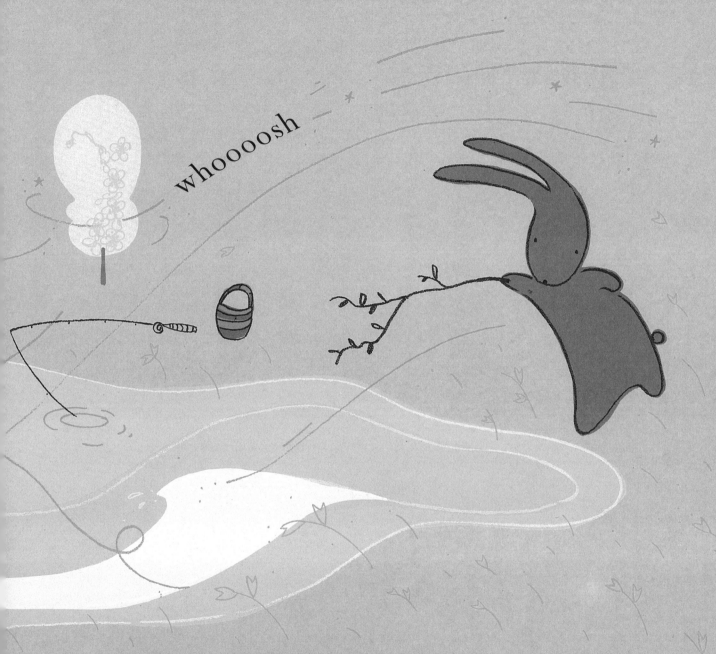

whooosh

Oh no! The wind has blown it
out of reach. Be careful Rust Rabbit!

Rose Rabbit is nearby,
hanging out her washing.

Ping!

Ping!

Look! Now her **orange** scarf has blown away.

Up everything flies.

Then down
it falls,

into the pond!

What's that tugging on Grey Rabbit's fishing line? Could it be a big fish?

No! He's caught . . .

. . . a **green** kite,

a **yellow** boat,

a **pink** bag,

a **blue** hat,

a **red** windmill,

and an **orange** scarf.

Heave-ho rabbits, reel them all in.
But everything is dripping wet!

Don't worry rabbits! There is room on the washing line, and on a windy day . . .

. . . everything will soon be dry.